celebrating twenty years

celebrating twenty years

BET Editors with
Marie Dutton Brown and Linda Tarrant-Reid
Written by David Earl Jackson

celebrating twenty years

Editorial Director Yanick Rice Lamb
Editors: Marie Dutton Brown and Linda Tarrant-Reid
Managing Editor: Kendra Lee
Writer: David Earl Jackson
Picture Editors: Paula Trotto and Rodd Vano
Copy Editor: Lisa A. Davis
Chief of Research: Carolyn Hardnett
Editorial Researchers: Tracy Harford, Knox Robinson, Gale Colden
Production Operations: Clarence Brown, Vice President;
Arline Williams, Director; EPI Communications, Rockville, Maryland
Design & Production: Giboire Media International Inc., New York City;
Clive Giboire, Art Director; Timothy Shamey, Designer & Timeline Art;
Craig Miller, Designer.
Corporate Communications: Michael Lewellyn, Vice President;
Gregory C. King, Director

BET BOOKS
Senior Vice President: Kelli Richardson
Publisher: Linda Gill Cater
Publishing Assistant: Kicheko Driggins
Business Affairs: Naomi Travers
Publicity: Julia Shaw, Shaw Literary Group

BET HOLDINGS, INC.
Chairman and CEO: Robert L. Johnson
President and COO: Debra L. Lee

Copyright © 2000 **BET Books**
Published by

BOOKS

1900 W Place, NE
Washington, DC 20018
www.BET.com

Book edition distributed by
Kensington Publishing Company c/o Penguin Putnam Inc.

First Edition
ISBN: 1-58314-191-X
Library of Congress Catalog Card Number: 00-101584

Printed in the United States of America

This book is dedicated to the artists and talent we have showcased
on our programs, in our films, magazines and books, and on our
Internet portal. We are proud to have provided you with a platform
to present your extraordinary gifts to the world. We recognize
that our success is the result of your success, and we invite
you to join us in creating the next 20 years.

CONTENTS

*Each Chapter Features a BET and African-American
Historic Highlights Timeline*

FOREWORD

DENZEL WASHINGTON, Academy Award-Winning Actor
Member of BET Holdings Inc. Board of Directors

Denzel Washington

THROUGH BLACK ENTERTAINMENT TELEVISION, WE'VE
moonwalked with Michael Jackson and walked that long road
to freedom with Nelson Mandela. One minute we're behind the
scenes in Hollywood; the next we're in the Oval Office at the White
House. We've been to "Frank's Place" and we've blasted into outer
space with astronaut Mae Jemison.

For two decades, BET has enlightened, empowered and enter-
tained us. It has provided a voice to the voiceless. It has painted a
vibrant portrait of people of African descent, highlighting our rich
hues. It has celebrated our triumphs while challenging us to
confront our shortcomings.

BET has helped our children savor the joy of reading. More
importantly, it has given them proof that they can reach for the
stars. They can see themselves on BET. They see people who look
like them calling the shots, taking a stand, breaking new ground.
They see us making history, preserving our culture, dropping
knowledge.

As a measure of balance, BET has presented a complete picture
of us to the world. It's a picture that is all too often blurred or distort-
ed in other media—if it exists at all. We recognize our picture on
BET, because we control the picture. We see the full breadth of our
experiences, not some one-dimensional image. We not only see
our great singers, but also our great thinkers analyzing the events
of the day. We see the fire in our faith and the strength of our families. We're reminded that we continue to be the most resilient
people on this planet.

Along with providing a complete picture, whether in news or
entertainment, BET has provided opportunities to create, to lead,
to soar. It has proven that "Black Star Power" exists on both sides
of the camera. Not all of our stars are on the air; many are behind
the scenes involved in investment, development, distribution and
other important areas.

BET has grown as a company as we have grown as a people. Its history mirrors our collective history—complete with the highs and lows. So as we celebrate BET, we celebrate ourselves. We have a shared legacy of excellence and empowerment, of beating the odds, of giving back, of standing the test of time.

BET means all of this and so much more. The same can be said of its founder, Robert L. Johnson. I'm honored to call Bob a friend and colleague. He's a true visionary who stands for what he believes in and believes in taking a stand. He did exactly that 20 years ago when he stood on his belief in us. He stood alone in believing that we deserved a cable channel catering to our tastes and showcasing a truer image of ourselves. While others said it wouldn't work, he believed that it could. And that channel grew into a network that has matured into a multimedia empire. Just as Bob bridged the gap on television in 1980, today, he's bridging the so-called digital divide on the Internet—and gaps everywhere in between, from the printed page to the silver screen.

Bob's dream has not only become reality, it has exceeded reality. This book tells that story. It describes the architect of the dream and the building of an institution—our institution. As we enter the new millennium, I'm proud to serve on BET's Board of Directors and to play a role in writing the next chapter of the BET story.

Happy anniversary, Black Entertainment Television. Here's to the next 20 years and beyond.

Denzel Washington

INTRODUCTION

From JOHN C. MALONE, Ph.D.

Chairman of the Board, Liberty Media Corporation

John C. Malone

NEARLY 20 YEARS AGO, BOB JOHNSON APPROACHED
me in the lobby of the National Cable Television Association
headquarters in Washington, D.C. Bob said he had an idea for a
cable network to serve the Black population, increasingly important to the cable industry as it sought to serve urban markets.

Bob was a one-man band when he started BET. He never
took his eye off the ball. Most people would have been too dis-
couraged and not had the patience to hang in there. But Bob
has incredible personal discipline. He's very serious about the
gift he has been given, to achieve something greater in his life-
time. And so, from our initial discussion, and through Bob's
incredible persistence, a great chapter in American entrepre-
neurship was written.

John C. Malone

FROM THE OFFICES OF
ROBERT L. JOHNSON
Founder, Chairman & CEO
DEBRA L. LEE
President & COO

Robert L. Johnson

SOMEWHERE IN THE WORLD, AT THIS VERY MOMENT, someone is enjoying a product from BET Holdings Inc. Maybe they are watching top-notch cable programming: the latest music video, a jazz or gospel concert, a thrilling made-for-television movie or a major motion picture, a hilarious stand-up comedy, a late-night talk show, or a stimulating roundtable discussion with high-powered journalists in the nation's capital. Or maybe they are dining at one of our SoundStage restaurants, or reading an article in *Heart & Soul* magazine about staying fit; staying on top of current events with *Emerge* magazine, or keeping track of Hollywood's hottest stars in the pages of *BET Weekend*. And now, absolutely anywhere in the world, they might be exploring the infinite world of the Internet and the ultimate convenience of e-commerce on BET.com.

When it comes to information and entertainment, BET Holdings Inc. is the multimedia company millions of people throughout the world turn to. That number is only going to increase. Two decades ago, BET was just a dream, an innovative idea seeking support. Now, with 20 years of solid cable programming as its foundation, BET is poised for groundbreaking growth in the 21st century. After decades of phenomenal success, it is a larger company with bigger dreams and more daring innovations. In many ways, we are just at the beginning of the story of BET. It is a wonderful story of striving and achievement. And it is a story that is getting better by the minute.

In January 1980, BET premiered with just two hours of music programming every Friday evening, reaching only 3.8 million cable subscribers in 350 markets across the country. Today, BET broadcasts a variety of programs 24 hours a day to 96 percent of the 7.6 million Black cable households in the United States. Out of 70 million cable households in the nation, BET is available in more than 60 million cable and satellite homes. BET is also seen throughout the Caribbean and in 13 other countries worldwide.

Debra L. Lee

BET's mission is clear: to become the preeminent diversified media company serving African-American consumers. It is that simple and that exciting.

BET is serious about the business of serving African-American consumers. On our own and in partnerships with other companies, we are offering products unique to our market, whether it is Arabesque Films, great music from BET on Jazz, award-winning magazines, or compelling interactive services.

BET is already a brand recognized by more than 95 percent of African-Americans; that is the kind of formidable leverage that will help us fulfill our mission to expand and comprehensively cover the information and media needs of African-American consumers. But that is just the tip of the iceberg.

BET, with its diverse outlets, is continually expanding into new avenues. It is the brand to trust. In the 21st century, we envision a multimedia company whose brand is so woven into the fabric of the life of African-American consumers that it will be synonymous with quality, respect and power.

BET Holdings Inc. is the company to watch for in the new millennium. Our solid foundation and commitment to our target market makes our future a bright and prosperous one. With our creative alliances with other corporations and our own innovative projects, we are poised to deliver quality products to our consumers in a comprehensive and dynamic way. You can always depend on BET's team to be on the lookout for new, exciting ways to bring goods and services to our target market, and to make sure we grasp every opportunity to better serve that market.

Our leadership team is the key to making the most of those opportunities. We are subscribers to the corporate doctrine that what determines a company's success is not the narrowness of its focus, but the quality of its management. We believe in the talent and dedication of our employees, who are working constantly to make sure we deliver the best possible product for our many loyal fans.

Robert L. Johnson　　*Debra L. Lee*

NEW STAR ON THE HORIZON

80·84

In the early years there were people who thought that Black Entertainment Television, with the emphasis on Black, was too narrow and was not a way for anyone to promote a business.

—**Robert L. Johnson,** BET Founder, Chairman & CEO

celebrating twenty years

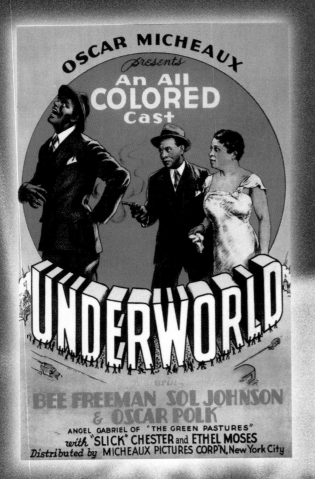

80·84

1980

January

Robert L. Johnson establishes Black Entertainment Television, a cable network in Washington, D.C. The network is targeted to African-Americans.

Robert L. Johnson

Six national corporations become BET charter advertisers.

BET premieres on January 25th to 3.8 million cable subscribers in 350 national markets.

May

BET allocates $1 million for Black collegiate sports and cable specials, the network's first venture into original programming.

November

BET adds two half-hour shows, "Bobby Jones Gospel" and "Black Showcase."

Bobby Jones

1981

January

BET celebrates its first anniversary with more than 5.3 million subscribers in 544 markets.

Nine corporations become major BET advertisers.

May

BET receives the Cable ACE Award for its Black college basketball coverage.

June

BET's "Video Soul" debuts.

1981—Historic Highlights
Bob Marley, 36, Jamaican reggae star and activist, dies of cancer in Miami.

Bob Marley

A Soldier's Play by Charles Fuller, 42, wins the Pulitzer Prize. It's his fourth play of The Negro Ensemble Company in New York.

David Bradley Jr.'s novel, *The Chaneysville Incident*, is published.

3.8 million subscribers

1984

8 million subscribers

January 1980

Toni Morrison

Toni Morrison's fourth novel, *Tar Baby*, is published. It follows *The Bluest Eye* (1970), *Sula* (1974) and *Song of Solomon* (1977).

The Heart of a Woman by Maya Angelou is published. It is the fourth volume of her autobiography, after *I Know Why the Caged Bird Sings* (1970), *Gather Together in My Name* (1974), and *Singin' and Swingin' and Gettin' Merry Like Christmas* (1976).

1982

February

Anheuser-Busch Inc. announces a multimillion-dollar, multi-year commitment to advertise on BET's new prime-time programming schedule.

August

BET switches to a new satellite, Westar, and begins broadcasting from 8 p.m. to 2 a.m., seven days a week, to 2 million national cable subscribers.

1982—Historic Highlights

Congress extends the Voting Rights Act of 1965 for 25 years.

Andrew Young, 49, becomes the second African-American mayor of Atlanta, succeeding Maynard Jackson, 51, the city's first Black mayor.

James Earl Jones, 51, stars in *Othello* on Broadway.

Michael Jackson's record-breaking album, *Thriller*, is released.

Alice Walker, 39, wins the Pulitzer Prize for her novel, *The Color Purple*.

1983

September

Home Box Office Inc. (HBO) becomes a BET minority equity partner.

BET begins televising six hours of music videos on "Video Soul."

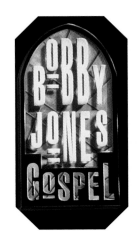

October

BET begins distributing its new 24-hour schedule to 7.6 million cable subscribers.

1983—Historic Highlights

Harold Washington, 60, is elected Chicago's first Black mayor.

Julius "Dr. J" Erving, 33, leads the Philadelphia 76ers to the National Basketball Association (NBA) championship.

The Rev. Dr. Martin Luther King Jr. holiday is established in the United States.

Lieutenant Colonel Guion S. Bluford Jr., 40, becomes the first African-American in space aboard the shuttle Challenger.

Michael Jackson

Vanessa L. Williams, 20, is crowned the first Black Miss America.

Robert C. Maynard, 46, becomes the first African-American owner of a major metropolitan daily newspaper in the United States, *The Oakland Tribune* in California. He was the newspaper's editor.

1984—Historic Highlights

The Rev. Jesse L. Jackson, 42, seeks the Democratic Nomination for President of the United States.

Michael Jordan, 21, debuts with the Chicago Bulls.

Carl Lewis, 23, wins four gold medals in track at the Los Angeles Olympics.

Arthur Ashe and Harry Belafonte found Artists & Athletes Against Apartheid.

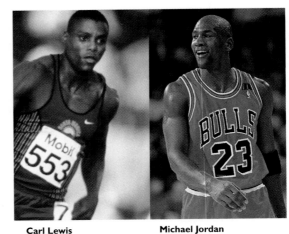

Carl Lewis   Michael Jordan

"A.M. Chicago," a daytime talk show, is renamed "The Oprah Winfrey Show." The program begins syndication in 1986.

David Bradley Jr.'s novel, *The Chaneysville Incident*, is published.

Trumpeter Wynton Marsalis, 22, wins Grammy Awards for jazz and classical recordings.

Harry Belafonte   Arthur Ashe

Wynton Marsalis   Oprah Winfrey

"The Cosby Show," starring Bill Cosby and Phylicia Rashad, premieres on NBC-TV.

Shirley Chisholm (D-N.Y.), 59, former Presidential candidate, establishes the National Political Congress of Black Women.

CHAPTER 1

NEW STAR ON THE HORIZON

On Friday, January 25, 1980, Robert L. Johnson sat with three associates and a small crew of technicians to ready the pioneering moment. They watched with anticipation, pride and excitement in a rented television studio in Alexandria, Virginia, as Black Entertainment Television made its historic broadcast debut. BET's first program was *A Visit to a Chief's Son*, a movie about a boy and his father on safari and the friendship that developed between the son and an African boy. "It was uplifting and pro-social—the right kind of thing for us in the early days," Johnson says. "Back then, most cable operators were in rural areas and were scared about what programming for the Black community would be all about."

Robert L. Johnson

It broadcast only two hours that Friday night from 11 p.m. to 1 a.m. "The feeling was 'Wow, this thing is happening!' This thing exists," Johnson recalls. "It was real at that point. We had been talking about it, and now suddenly it was real."

Today BET, the nation's first and only Black-owned cable channel, is an ever-expanding network star in the cable television galaxy.

In 20 years, the company's subscriber base has grown from 3.8 million households to more than 60 million in the United States, Canada, Africa, Asia and Europe. The cable network has evolved into a multimedia empire. BET Holdings Inc. consists of five cable networks, six magazines, an African-American romance novel imprint, three entertainment-themed restaurants and a nightclub, a film division, a movie studio and the ultimate

Internet portal for African-Americans. The market value of this media conglomerate is estimated at more than $2 billion.

BET ROLLS THE DICE

In the early days, many Black media observers considered the Black cable upstart a gamble. Even more skeptics predicted BET's failure.

But Johnson was passionate about his belief in his network. He had seen cable television's future, and the possibility for a Black-oriented cable network in the 1970s, when he was vice president of government relations for the National Cable Television Association (NCTA), a trade association representing cable television companies.

From his perspective at NCTA, Johnson could see that scores of new programming services were scrambling to challenge the traditional broadcast networks. And cable operators were also beginning to apply for franchises to wire urban markets.

Johnson surmised that African-Americans watched more television during the average week than other groups of people. Johnson also knew that the Black population was growing at twice the rate of the White population and that African-

John C. Malone

Americans represented a quarter of a trillion dollars in combined earned income. And finally, he knew that network television was not addressing the interests and concerns of African-American viewers. Armed with this powerful information, Johnson aimed for his target and started working his plan.

He discussed starting a Black network with John C. Malone, who was on the NCTA board and president and CEO of TeleCommunications Inc. (TCI). Malone had been trying, unsuccessfully, to import Black programs to Memphis, where 50 percent of Black Tennesseans lived and where TCI had a system. Malone told Johnson that if he ever wanted to start a network, TCI would support him with cable carriage and financial support.

MALONE STEPS IN

In 1979, Johnson quit NCTA and took out a personal loan of $15,000 while he laid the foundation for Black Entertainment Television. Before approaching Malone, he conducted further research and scheduled satellite time. He also met with Bob Rosencrans, president of UA/Columbia Cablevision, about his idea. Rosencrans, an early supporter of HBO and a co-founder of C-SPAN, leased Johnson two hours a week, from 11 p.m. to 1 a.m., on Madison Square Garden's transponder.

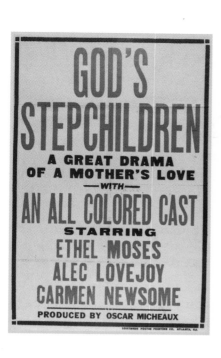

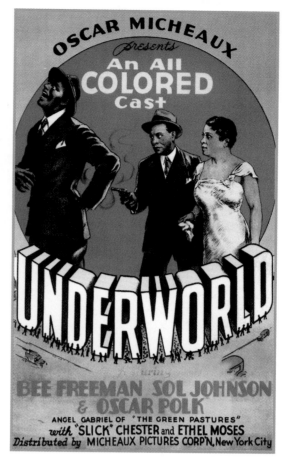

Posters of movies
aired on BET

Johnson announced the creation of BET on August 8, 1979, and secured agreements from Warner Cable, TelePrompTer and American Telecommunications Corporation. He then went back to Malone. On the strength of Johnson's vision, Malone invested $180,000 and loaned Johnson an additional $320,000. TCI owned 20 percent of the company, with Johnson owning 80 percent. This $500,000 launched the Black Entertainment Television network.

"I was nervous. I got that check and that was more money than I had ever seen in my life," Johnson says. "I figured the plane was going to crash on the way back. Something had to happen."

With TCI on board, Johnson set out to improve distribution. It would not be hard. "Operators wanted urban programming to make them attractive as prospective franchise-holders," Johnson recalls. "I remember sitting down with all of the operators who were competing for Pittsburgh—and each one wanted to be the first to put out a press release that they'd signed to carry BET."

Switching careers is common today—with versatility and risk as the watchwords—but 20 years ago it wasn't something your typical African-American professional considered. But Robert L. Johnson was not average. A graduate of the University of Illinois, with a master's degree in public affairs from the Woodrow Wilson School of Public and International Affairs at Princeton University, Johnson served as press secretary for the

Honorable Walter E. Fauntroy, Congressional delegate from the District of Columbia, before joining NCTA. He held earlier positions at the Washington, D.C. Urban League and at the Corporation for Public Broadcasting.

BUILDING PARTNERSHIPS

Besides using his business savvy, Johnson built BET on strategic partnerships with such diverse companies as TCI Inc. (now AT&T Broadband and Internet Services), Taft Broadcasting Company and HBO.

In addition, six national companies signed on as charter advertisers: Anheuser-Busch; Time; Champale; Pepsi Cola; Sears-Roebuck & Company and Kellogg. These advertisers provided a stream of income that was critical in the network's first year.

Working with three people out of a three-room office at 3222 N Street, N.W., in Washington, Johnson was busy. "I did everything but run a camera," he explains. "I produced shows. I wrote copy. I did interviews. I sold advertising time. I sold affiliate sales. I handled the banking relationships."

Within five months of the cable network's debut, BET allocated $1 million to produce Black collegiate sports broadcasts and specials—its first foray into original programming. Johnson even interviewed presidents of Historically Black Colleges and Universities (HBCUs) during half-time.

Paul Robeson as *Emperor Jones*

Lena Horne in *Stormy Weather*

Dr. Bobby Jones

During its early years, BET showed many movies with all-Black casts made by independent filmmakers for Black audiences, from the silent-film era through the 1940s. BET introduced its viewers to the films of the legendary filmmaker Oscar Micheaux. BET also showcased such all-Black musicals as *Stormy Weather* and *Cabin in the Sky*. And the network aired such popular contemporary classics as *Lady Sings the Blues, Sparkle* and *Greased Lightning*.

In less than a year, the young network increased its subscriber count by more than one million viewers and expanded its original programming, adding two new shows: "Bobby Jones Gospel" and "Black Showcase," a celebrity profile show. By the fall of 1980, BET was serving five million cable households in 47 states, including Alaska and Hawaii.

As one of the first programs on BET's schedule, "Bobby Jones Gospel" reigns as the most consistently popular program on the network. Debuting in November 1980, "Bobby Jones Gospel" is also the longest-running weekly show in cable television history. Hosted by Jones, the program's high ratings have been critical to building BET's numbers. Jones has become one of gospel music's most influential personalities and visible leaders. Every Sunday, Jones and the New Life Singing Aggregation have steadfastly kept contemporary gospel music in the spotlight, presenting artists as varied as Albertina Walker, Yolanda Adams, the Canton Spirituals, Kirk Franklin, John P. Kee and Hezekiah Walker to a new audience of viewers.

Bobby Jones Gospel

BET SUPPORTS BLACK COLLEGE SPORTS

Other programming broadcast on BET in the early years was Black college sports. BET was filling a void for its viewers left by network television's refusal to give HBCUs the same exposure given other National Collegiate Athletic Association colleges and universities. BET remains the only network to provide regular coverage of HBCU sporting events.

BET has given African-American viewers the opportunity to witness HBCUs on the field and the gridiron strategy of such legendary coaches as Eddie Robinson of Grambling University in Grambling, Louisiana, the "winningest" coach in the history of college football. For many viewers, BET has been the primary media outlet to showcase the unique tradition of Black college cheerleaders and marching bands, such as The Sonic Boom of Jackson State University and the Marching "100" of Florida A&M, squaring off as fiercely as their respective football teams.

On May 31, 1981, BET won the first of many awards for excellence. The National Cable Television Association (NCTA) honored BET with its Cable ACE Award for its Black college sports coverage.

Black College Sports on the gridiron

Shalamar

Midnight Starr

THE STAR SHINES ON MUSIC

A half-hour music program debuted on BET on June 26, 1981. "Video Soul" featured music videos by Earth, Wind & Fire, the Whispers, Shalamar, Midnight Starr and Luther Vandross. The program also featured interviews with top recording artists and a "behind-the-scenes" look at the music industry. "Video Soul" jumped out front right away as one of BET's most-popular programs, solidifying the use of music videos as the anchor of the network's programming format. The popular Washington radio personality, Donnie Simpson, became "Video Soul" host in 1983. BET would eventually be credited with premiering the early work of En Vogue, R. Kelly, Erykah Badu, Mary J. Blige, Maxwell and Boyz II Men. Mariah Carey's first national interview was on "Video Soul."

Whitney Houston was also on BET in the early days. "I remember going to the tiny station up there," Whitney reminisces. "It was a little old thing. One building. I had 'You Give Good Love.' I watched BET grow as well as myself. They helped me to grow. I've watched BET nurture African-American entertainers."

BET's star shone brightly the following year when the company expanded its music programming, building the weekly half-hour "Video Soul" into a six-hour block every week that included music videos, interviews and increased coverage of the music industry. This expansion followed the wave of Michael Jackson's phenomenal 1982 breakthrough album, *Thriller*, and the three surreal and innovative companion music-and-dance videos, "Beat It," "Billie Jean"—as well as the epic "Thriller."

Earth, Wind & Fire

These videos helped to sell more than 40 million copies of the *Thriller* album worldwide and ushered in the music video age. Jackson's videos broke down the door for the acceptance of other Black music videos, destroying the color barrier at other cable outlets that had discriminated against Black musical products.

Run-DMC

BET's programming of Black music videos garnered the loyalty of young fans and baby boomers alike, just as it had with collegiate sports. Johnson understood that music is the dominant cultural expression in African-American society. And as the only African-American entertainment network, BET would have been remiss if it had not provided viewers with balanced music programming—from gospel to jazz to R&B to hip-hop.

Another important musical milestone came later that year when Run-DMC's self-titled album on Profile Records went gold. The popularity of this rap act signaled that the market for hip-hop and rap was expanding into a multimillion dollar industry.

"BET helped develop Kurtis Blow, Run-DMC, Whodini and all the early rap artists," says Russell Simmons, the rap and hip-hop pioneer. "They were critical to the expansion of hip-hop culture."

The entertainment entrepreneur further believes that BET will play a critical role in the expansion and preservation of hip-hop, blues and jazz, as well as rock and roll. "You've got to look to them to preserve those art forms in their most honest forms," Simmons says. "The early artists have had integrity in the way they deliver their art forms, and there is a lot of commercialism and influences that change it from its core. BET will protect its core."

The history of music videos and BET's musical programming goes back to Hollywood musicals and "soundies" from the 1940s—jukeboxes with pictures. But the true forerunners of the videos so commonplace today were the promotional clips of artists who were too busy to make personal appearances. Record companies started shooting "promos" in the 1960s and 1970s and supplying them to television programs, clubs and other outlets. In the early 1980s, the record industry was losing money: Disco had peaked, and radio was not "making" hits like it once had been able to do. Music videos and the new television outlets that aired them proved to be the ideal solution. BET caught this wave and rode it to popularity, influence and wealth.

At the end of the first five years, BET's star was clearly visible, reflecting its growth in stature in the cable television industry. This so-called "Black cable gamble" was staying steady on the course that Robert Johnson had charted, becoming one of the most-valued consumer brands within the Black marketplace.

BET 100 BEST VIDEOS OF THE 20TH CENTURY

 **A**

Dr. Martin Luther King Jr.   I Have a Dream

B

A. Michael Jackson **B.** Busta Rhymes **C.** Marvin Gaye **D.** Dr. Dre
E. Run-DMC with Aerosmith **F.** TLC

D

F

A. Janet Jackson   **B.** Hammer   **C.** Herbie Hancock   **D.** Tupac Shakur

BET'S TOP 100 VIDEOS OF THE 20TH CENTURY

1. **Martin Luther King Jr.** I Have a Dream
2. **Michael Jackson** Thriller
3. **Busta Rhymes** Woo-Hah!
4. **Marvin Gaye** Sexual Healing
5. **Dr. Dre** Nuthin' But a "G" Thang
6. **Michael Jackson** Beat It
7. **Run-DMC/Aerosmith** Walk This Way
8. **TLC** Waterfalls
9. **Janet Jackson** Rhythm Nation
10. **MC Hammer** U Can't Touch This
11. **Herbie Hancock** Rockit

12. **2Pac featuring Dr. Dre** California Love
13. **DJ Jazzy Jeff and the Fresh Prince**
    Parents (Just Don't Understand)
14. **Michael Jackson** Billie Jean
15. **Notorious B.I.G.** Mo' Money, Mo' Problems
16. **Bone Thugs-N-Harmony** Crossroads
17. **Prince** When Doves Cry
18. **USA for Africa** We Are the World
19. **Stop the Violence Movement**
    Self Destruction
20. **Naughty By Nature** Hip Hop Hooray

A. DJ Jazzy Jeff & the Fresh Prince   **B.** Notorious B.I.G. & Puffy   **C.** Bone Thugs-N-Harmony
D. Prince   **E.** Naughty By Nature   **F.** N.W.A.

A. Earth, Wind & Fire   B. LL Cool J   C. Brandy & Monica   D. Coolio
E. George Clinton   F. Grand Master Flash

A. Lionel Richie   **B.** Fugees   **C.** New Edition   **D.** Wreckx-N-Effect
E. Boyz II Men   **F.** En Vogue

A

B

C

D

A. R. Kelly   **B.** Whitney Houston   **C.** DeBarge   **D.** Will Smith

BET'S TOP 100 VIDEOS OF THE 20TH CENTURY

21. **Michael & Janet Jackson** Scream
22. **N.W.A.** Express Yourself
23. **Earth, Wind & Fire** Let's Groove
24. **LL Cool J** I'm Bad
25. **Brandy & Monica** The Boy Is Mine
26. **Coolio** Gangsta's Paradise
27. **Michael Jackson** Remember the Time
28. **Missy Elliott** The Rain
29. **TLC** Creep
30. **Public Enemy** Fight the Power
31. **Notorious B.I.G.** One More Chance

32. **George Clinton & Parliament/Funkadelic**
    Atomic Dog
33. **Craig Mack** Flava in Your Ear (remix)
34. **Grandmaster Flash and the Furious Five**
    The Message
35. **Lionel Richie** All Night Long
36. **Fugees** Killing Me Softly With His Song
37. **Michael Jackson** Bad
38. **Janet Jackson** If
39. **Busta Rhymes** Put Your Hands Where
    My Eyes Could See

A. Snoop Doggy Dogg   B. Missy Elliott   C. Public Enemy   D. D'Angelo
E. Erykah Badu   F. Tina Turner

40. **New Edition** Cool It Now
41. **Salt -N- Pepa** Push It
42. **Bobby Brown** My Perogative
43. **Wreckx-n-Efect** Rump Shaker
44. **Boyz II Men** End of the Road
45. **TLC** Ain't Too Proud to Beg
46. **DJ Jazzy Jeff and the Fresh Prince**
    Summertime
47. **En Vogue** Free Your Mind
48. **Method Man featuring Mary J. Blige**
    I'll Be There for You/You're All I Need
49. **R. Kelly** Down Low
50. **D'Angelo** Brown Sugar
51. **Whitney Houston** I'll Always Love You
52. **DeBarge** Rhythm of the Night
53. **Janet Jackson** Pleasure Principle
54. **Salt -N- Pepa** Whatta Man
55. **Will Smith** Wild Wild West
56. **2Pac** Keep Your Head Up
57. **Lionel Richie** Hello
58. **Prince** Kiss
59. **Snoop Doggy Dogg** Gin & Juice
60. **Arrested Development** Tennessee
61. **Chaka Khan** I Feel For You
62. **Tina Turner** What's Love Got to Do With It
63. **Janet Jackson** Again
64. **En Vogue** My Lovin' (You're Never
    Gonna Get it)
65. **Michael Jackson** The Way You Make
    Me Feel
66. **Kid 'N Play** 2 Hype
67. **LL Cool J** Mama Said Knock You Out
68. **Stevie Wonder** Part-Time Lover
69. **Lauryn Hill** Doo-Wop (That Thing)

70. **Tone-Loc** Wild Thing
71. **C + C Music Factory** Gonna Make
    You Sweat
72. **Milli Vanilli** Girl, You Know It's True
73. **Kriss Kross** Jump
74. **Erykah Badu** On & On
75. **Force MD's** Tender Love
76. **Mary J. Blige** Real Love
77. **Michael Jackson** Jam
78. **Montell Jordan** This is How We Do It
79. **Slick Rick** Children's Story
80. **Lil' Kim** Crush On You
81. **Boyz II Men** I'll Make Love to You
82. **Janet Jackson** Alright
83. **Sade** Sweetest Taboo
84. **LL Cool J** Goin' Back to Cali
85. **A Tribe Called Quest** Scenario
86. **Eric B & Rakim** I Ain't No Joke
87. **Paula Abdul** Straight Up
88. **Public Enemy** Night of the Living
    Baseheads
89. **Digital Underground** Humpty Dance
90. **Prince** 1999
91. **TLC** No Scrubs
92. **Bobby Brown** Don't Be Cruel
93. **Rockwell** Somebody's Watching Me
94. **Xzibit** What U See is What U Get
95. **New Edition** If It Isn't Love
96. **Puff Daddy** It's All About the Benjamins
97. **Soul II Soul** Back to Life
98. **Will Smith** Men in Black
99. **Janet Jackson** Nasty
100. **Sugarhill Gang** Rapper's Delight

BLACK STAR RISING

Black people have always needed their own voice, their own forum, their own platform from which to proclaim to all the world just how it goes with us. Black Entertainment Television provides us with such an arena.

—Ossie Davis, Actor/Activist

celebrating *20* twenty years

1985

January

BET celebrates its fifth anniversary with 8 million subscribers.

April

Robert L. Johnson announces a sales and marketing agreement with HBO.

1985—Historic Highlights

"We Are the World," produced by Quincy Jones with many top entertainers, raises millions of dollars in aid for African famine victims.

Gwendolyn Brooks, 67, the first African-American writer to win a Pulitzer Prize (1950), is named Poet Laureate of the United States.

Eddie G. Robinson, 66, coach of the Grambling State University Tigers, sets the record for winning the most games in college football.

1986

August

BET introduces "Video LP," featuring BET's first female VJ, Sherry Carter.

October

Robert L. Johnson announces at the Congressional Black Caucus Convention the debut of "BET News," America's first Black national news program.

1986—Historic Highlights

Bishop Desmond M. Tutu of South Africa, 54, wins the Martin Luther King Jr. Nonviolent Peace Prize.

Congress passes The Comprehensive Anti-Apartheid Act of 1986, overriding the veto of President Ronald Reagan.

Spike Lee, 29, makes his directorial and acting debut in the independent film *She's Gotta Have It.*

Sherry Carter

Mike Tyson, 20, wins the heavyweight boxing championship, becoming the youngest man ever to win the title.

23 million subscribers

1986

1984

3.8 million subscribers

ON AIR

ROBERT JOHNSON

January 1980

8 million subscribers

1989

17.4 million subscribers

1987

January

BET conducts a national telephone survey of attitudes toward "Amos 'N Andy," the controversial CBS television series of the 1950s.

Cheryl Martin, BET News

November

BET's subscriber base reaches 17.4 million in 1,000 markets.

1987—Historic Highlights

Kurt Schmoke, 37, becomes Baltimore's first Black-elected mayor.

Johnnetta B. Cole, Ph.D., 51, becomes the first African-American female president of Spelman College in Atlanta.

Benjamin S. Carson, M.D., 36, a Baltimore neurosurgeon, makes medical history performing the first successful separation of Siamese twins joined at the head.

Reginald F. Lewis, 44, chief executive officer of the Lewis Company (TLC), masterminds the $985 million buyout of Beatrice International Foods Inc., creating the nation's largest Black-owned company.

August Wilson's Broadway play, *Fences*, wins a Tony Award.

1988

December

Robert L. Johnson announces new and aggressive programming strategies for BET, including the premiere of nine shows produced by BET for the 1989–1990 fall season.

1988—Historic Highlights

The Rev. Jesse L. Jackson makes his second attempt to win the Democratic Presidential nomination.

Jesse Jackson

The 25th anniversary of the 1963 March on Washington.

Carl Lewis, Florence Griffith-Joyner and Jackie Joyner-Kersee sweep the track-and-field events at the Olympics in Seoul, Korea.

1989

April

Robert L. Johnson officially opens BET's $10 million production facility.

June

BET's subscriber base reaches 23 million in 1,300 markets.

August

BET and Butch Lewis Productions Inc. present the first championship boxing match to be televised on BET.

Butch Lewis

Florence Griffith-Joyner

1989—Historic Highlights
General Colin L. Powell, 52, becomes the youngest and the first African-American Chairman of the Joint Chiefs of Staff.

Colin Powell

David N. Dinkins, 62, is elected the first African-American mayor of New York City.

Art Shell, 43, becomes the first African-American to coach a National Football League team, the Oakland Raiders.

Ron Brown

Ronald H. Brown, 48, is elected Chairman of the Democratic National Committee, becoming the first African-American to lead a major U.S. political party.

L. Douglas Wilder

L. Douglas Wilder, 58, is elected the first Black governor of Virginia.

CHAPTER 2

BLACK STAR RISING

T hose monitoring the cable television galaxy could see that this network's rising star was shining brightly. BET celebrated its fifth anniversary in 1985 with an increase to more than eight million subscribers. BET was moving toward its destiny as the most-valued brand among Black consumers. By spring, the network had signed a new marketing and sales agreement with HBO.

BET benefited early on from its partnership with HBO and Time-Warner, according to Curtis Symonds, BET's executive vice president of affiliate sales and marketing.

"Time-Warner and HBO had a couple of African-American executives working for them," Symonds recalls. "At the time, BET didn't have the budget, nor the staff, to do the affiliate work. Don Anderson got things going on that side, dealing with the cable operators. The network had been out there two or three years when he first got involved. At the time, most cable operators were paying about a penny per subscriber per month, which was very low. The rates eventually went up to two cents over four years. There was a raise in the fee to five cents in January 1989, increasing one cent a year until 1994."

"When HBO came in 1983 as an investor and was helping out with our affiliate sales," Johnson recalls, "we felt we had to push more programming out there if we were going to justify the five-cent fee. So we started looking at program concepts that includ-

Ed Gordon

Cheryl Martin

ed more in-studio shows and fewer music-based programs. That was all part of trying to make a case for the increase."

"If you go back and look at these shows, they all had to meet a certain criteria," Johnson continues. "I had something called three-ins: in the studio, in the can or in existence. In the studio was a public affairs show. In the can was movies, like *Lady Sings the Blues*, *Sparkle* and *Blue Collar*. In existence was anything that was already happening, like Black college football or basketball. That's the way we programmed it."

A TIME FOR EXPANSION: BET NEWS

In 1986 BET expanded its original programming further with "Video LP." The 30-minute show featured BET's first female VJ, Sherry Carter. She had co-hosted "Soul Soundtrax," a music-

Ed Gordon with Ron Brown

video show in Cleveland. On "Video LP," Carter reported for the show's weekly "In the Groove" segment. She moved on to co-host "Video Soul Top 20" with Donnie Simpson and to perform voice-overs for "Video Soul by Request."

At the 16th Annual Congressional Black Caucus Convention, Johnson made a major announcement. He told the attendees of the October 10, 1986, debut of "BET News," America's first national Black news program. Johnson had hired Deborah Tang to organize BET's news department that August. "When I started at BET," Tang says, "they were doing a two-minute cut-in three or four times a day. That was their news. They wanted to have a national newscast at least once a week. They wanted to make sure BET could cover the Democratic and Republican conventions that were coming up in 1988. That was when Jesse Jackson was running for President. It was a very exciting time."

"BET News" was originally hosted by Paul Berry, an anchor for the ABC affiliate station in Washington. Tang was executive producer. About the same time she also launched "On the Line," a telephone call-in show hosted by Doris McMillon.

The news and public affairs division later evolved to include such programs as "For the Record With the Congressional Caucus," "Conversations With Ed Gordon," "BET Tonight With Tavis Smiley," "Lead Story," "Teen Summit" and "Heart & Soul."

Among the most memorable shows Tang produced was "Our Voices," hosted by Bev Smith. "'Our Voices' took on a life of its own," Tang recalls. "Bev was a very strong talent, and the program received really good numbers. At one point, 'Our Voices' came on five nights a week."

In September 1987, BET launched its first national consumer-awareness campaign in the top 20 targeted markets. It reached more than five million BET viewers and 1.8 million new subscribers. By November 1, 1987, BET's subscriber base had expanded to 17.4 million in 1,000 markets. The next year, Johnson announced an aggressive programming strategy that included the premiere of nine original shows in the 1989–1990 season.

On April 1, 1989, BET opened its new $10 million production operation in Washington's northeast corridor, and by June 1, the network's subscriber base had grown to 23 million in 1,300 markets.

Tavis Smiley

Bev Smith

Tavis Smiley and
Vice President Al Gore

BET WALK
OF FAME

BET WALK OF FAME

THE BET WALK OF FAME WAS ESTABLISHED IN 1995 to honor entertainers who have made an outstanding contribution to the music industry. Bronze plaques with the entertainer's name and a star are installed into the walk in front of BET's Corporate Headquarters, bringing a little bit of Hollywood to Washington, D.C.

The inductees are honored at a Walk of Fame Gala, which features entertainment by the inductee and other performers. The Gala is an annual event benefiting the UNCF's College Fund. Nearly $1 million has been raised for scholarships since the Walk of Fame's inception.

THE WALK OF FAME HONOREES ARE:

September 22, 1995	Michael Jackson
September 13, 1996	Whitney Houston
October 3, 1997	Kenneth "Babyface" Edmonds
October 23, 1998	Boyz II Men
October 23, 1999	Diana Ross

"Bob Johnson and his wife, Sheila, have always been supporters of The College Fund. In five years, they have raised almost one million dollars for young people from the African-American community to attend UNCF colleges."

—WILLIAM GRAY
    President and CEO,
    The College Fund/UNCF

MICHAEL
JACKSON

Walk of Fame

Black Entertainment Television Walk of Fame
dedicated to those artists and to their creative genius
- the foundation upon which BET stands.

- Robert L. Johnson
Chairman/Founder BET Holdings, Inc.
September 15, 1995.

WHITNEY HOUSTON

Walk of Fame

Black Entertainment Television Walk of Fame
dedicated to those artists and to their creative genius
– the foundation upon which BET stands.

Robert L. Johnson
Chairman/Founder BET Holdings, Inc.
September 15, 1993.

K E N N E T H
" B A B Y F A C E "
E D M O N D S

Black Entertainment Television Walk of Fame
dedicated to those artists and to their creative genius
- the foundation upon which BET stands.

- Robert L. Johnson
Chairman/Founder BET Holdings, Inc.
September 15, 1995.

BOYZ II MEN

Black Entertainment Television Walk of Fame
dedicated to those artists and to their creative genius
- the foundation upon which BET stands.

- Robert L. Johnson
Chairman/Founder BET Holdings, Inc.
September 15, 1995.

DIANA
ROSS

Black Entertainment Television Walk of Fame
dedicated to those artists and to their creative genius
the foundation upon which BET stands.

Robert L. Johnson
Chairman/Founder BET Holdings, Inc.
September 15, 1995.

53

"BET has provided a service for the Black entertainment industry. It has provided a unique platform for entertainers who otherwise might not have gotten an opportunity to be viewed nationally and also to have a stage upon which to entertain. BET has been a source of pride and interest to African-Americans because of the fact that they have been able to see feature films and productions that relate to them. The overwhelming part of our community is positive and BET has tried to bring that out."

—WILLIAM GRAY

BET GIVES BACK

Sheila Johnson

OF BET's many philanthropic projects, Urban Nation Voices of Youth H.I.P. H.O.P. Choir is the one nearest and dearest to the heart of Sheila Johnson, executive vice president of corporate affairs. The acronym, H.I.P. H.O.P., in the choir's name stands for Hope, Integrity, Power—Helping Our People. "This is a choir to get kids off the street, get them out of trouble, to provide a creative outlet that's positive—something other than sex and drugs and hanging out on the corner," Mrs. Johnson explains. "We want these young people to recapture their spiritual health. And once they recapture that, they can start focusing on themselves and what is important, and setting goals for themselves. So far, this choir has helped almost 200 kids."

AIDS. ILLITERACY. TEEN PREGNANCY.

These are just a few of the community issues that BET has tried to address through volunteer efforts, in-kind services and donations to charities and organizations exceeding more than $1 million each year. "We have given more than $3 million in funds strictly for youth causes," estimates Sheila Johnson. One such fundraising event is "A Celebration of Self-Help," which was co-sponsored by "BET News" and the Children's Defense Fund for the Black Community Crusade for Children.

EXPANDING THE GALAXY

90·94

It takes keen insight and innate business acumen to maintain such a successful and prolific multimedia company. Bob Johnson has demonstrated such prowess and has proved to the world that he can, indeed, play with the big boys.

—Edward Lewis, Chairman, Publisher and CEO
Essence Communications Inc.

celebrating twenty years

TURNING AWAY IMMIGRANTS ■ ENVIRONMENTAL RACISM

BLACK AMERICA'S NEWSMAGAZINE

emerge

The Death of
EMMETT TILL
A Mother's
40-Year Agony

"Powerful!
One of the most important
films I've seen this year!"
—ROGER EBERT, *Chicago Sun-Times*

90·94

1990

January

BET debuts "Frank's Place," the Emmy Award-winning series starring Tim Reid and Daphne Maxwell Reid.

Quincy Jones   **Denzel Washington**

Thurgood Marshall   **Clarence Thomas**

September

BET forms United Image Entertainment Inc. with Tim Reid and Butch Lewis to produce quality films for African-Americans.

October

BET's subscriber base jumps to 29.1 million in 2,400 markets.

1990—Historic Highlights

Political activist Nelson Mandela tours the United States and addresses Congress after his release from prison in South Africa after 27 years.

President George Bush vetoes the Civil Rights Bill of 1990, saying it imposes quota systems.

Quincy Jones, 57, wins five Grammy Awards.

Denzel Washington, 35, wins the Academy Award for Best Supporting Actor for his performance in *Glory*.

1991

January

BET subscriber base reaches 30 million.

May

BET acquires Time Warner Inc.'s ownership stake in *Emerge*, giving the network controlling interest in the newsmagazine.

August

YSB publishes its first issue with a circulation of 150,000.

23 million subscribers

17.4 million subscribers

1989

1986

1984

3.8 million subscribers

8 million subscribers

January 1980

ON AIR

ROBERT JOHNSON

October

BET sells stock to the public in an initial public offering, becoming the first Black-owned company to be listed on the New York Stock Exchange.

1991—Historic Highlights

Rodney King is beaten by four White Los Angeles Police Department (L.A.P.D.) officers. The beating is captured on home video and is transmitted on television, sparking outrage across the country.

Thurgood Marshall, 83, retires after 24 years as a Justice of the U.S. Supreme Court.

Clarence Thomas, 43, is nominated by President George Bush to fill the U.S. Supreme Court vacancy left by the retiring Marshall. He is later confirmed by Congress.

Terry McMillan

May

BET airs an exclusive interview with President George Bush following his survey of Los Angeles after the riots caused by the Rodney King verdict.

39.1 million subscribers

1994

1992

April

BET airs an exclusive interview with former Mayor Marion S. Barry Jr. of Washington, D.C., from a federal prison in Loreto, Pennsylvania, as part of its "Conversations With Ed Gordon" series.

"BET News" presents "The Verdict and the Violence," a special examining the controversial acquittal of the four L.A.P.D. officers accused of beating Rodney King.

Mae C. Jemison

September

BET announces its first National Teachers Grant Competition winners.

November

BET signs its first Canadian affiliate in Yellow Knife, Northwest Territory.

1992—Historic Highlights

Terry McMillan's blockbuster novel, *Waiting to Exhale*, is published.

Spike Lee's epic, *Malcolm X*, is released.

Carol Mosley Braun (D.-Ill.), 45, becomes the first African-American woman elected to the U.S. Senate.

Derek Alton Walcott, 62, the Caribbean-born poet, becomes the first Black to win the Nobel Prize for Literature.

Mae C. Jemison, M.D., 35, becomes the first African-American woman in space aboard shuttle Endeavour.

1993

May

BET is recognized by *Business Week* as one of the nation's 100 Best Small Corporations in the annual "Hot Growth Companies" issue.

BET announces a ground-breaking ceremony for a new corporate headquarters in northeast Washington.

90·94

90·94

June

BET announces plans to purchase 80 percent of Action Pay-Per-View.

BET holds its first "Unity Day" celebration in Oakland, California.

July

BET is available in Europe for the first time via a venture with Identity Television.

August

BET forms BET International™, providing network programming to Africa and other world markets.

September

BET announces the creation of BET on Jazz: The Cable Jazz Channel™.

December

BET announces the development of BET Film Productions, a partnership with Encore, the premium cable service, and LIVE Entertainment, a home-video company.

BET and the Blockbuster Entertainment Corporation agree to a partnership called BET Pictures.

1993—Historic Highlights

Arthur Ashe, 49, tennis champion and human rights activist, dies.

Toni Morrison, 62, becomes the first African-American to receive the Nobel Prize for Literature.

Nelson Mandela accepts the Nobel Peace Prize.

Reginald F. Lewis, 50, chief executive officer of TLC Beatrice International, dies.

Robert C. Maynard, 56, *Oakland Tribune* owner, dies.

Innovative jazz trumpeter and composer Dizzy Gillespie, 75, dies.

Legendary crooner Billy Eckstine, 78, dies.

Marian Anderson, the pioneering operatic contralto, dies at age 93.

1994

January

BET reaches 39.1 million homes.

BET's "Teen Summit" wins the first of five NAACP Image Award for "Teens & AIDS."

February

BET airs an exclusive interview with Minister Louis Farrakhan of the Nation of Islam.

BET simulcasts *Race to Freedom: The Underground Railroad* with the Family Channel in recognition of Black History Month.

March

BET holds a Mandela Freedom Fund Telethon to support South Africa's change to a democratic form of government.

BET is recognized by Childhelp USA as one of America's "101 Corporate Heroes" and is honored for its "Teen Summit" and "StoryPorch" programs.

July

BET signs an agreement with Comsat Video Enterprises Inc. The deal gives BET the potential to reach more than 300,000 hotel rooms in the United States.

November

BET presents "President Clinton and Black Americans Face-to-Face."

1994—Historic Highlights

Former professional football player O.J. Simpson, 46, is charged with two murders in Los Angeles, resulting in "The Trial of the Century."

Nelson Mandela, 76, is inaugurated as the first democratically elected Black African President of the Republic of South Africa.

EXPANDING THE GALAXY

I n January 1990, BET celebrated its 10th anniversary with more than 25 million subscribers in 50 states. The network debuted "Frank's Place," an Emmy Award-winning CBS series starring Tim Reid and Daphne Maxwell Reid. That March, BET formed a partnership with Butch Lewis Productions to produce original programming and pay-per-view special events for the network.

Best known as a boxing promoter, Butch Lewis' crowning jewel is the three-hour pay-per-view James Brown musical special he produced with BET in 1990. This historic broadcast, following Brown's release from prison, featured MC Hammer and other stars paying tribute to the Godfather of Soul.

That year, BET, Lewis and Tim Reid also formed United Image Entertainment (UIE) to produce feature films. "We founded United Image Entertainment with the simple intent to make the kind of movies about the African-American experience that Hollywood refused to consider," Reid says. "It is safe to say that without BET's involvement, the films UIE has produced would not have been made."

From this venture came the critically acclaimed *Out of Sync*, *Race to Freedom: The Underground Railroad* and *Once Upon a Time . . . When We Were Colored*.

Race to Freedom was co-produced for BET and The Family Channel by UIE and Atlantis Films. It was simulcast by both networks during Black History Month in 1994. The drama starred Courtney Vance, Dawnn Lewis and Glynn Turman and chronicled the lives of two young runaway slaves who escaped from a plantation to Canada through the Underground Railroad.

Daphne Maxwell Reid & Tim Reid

"Powerful!
One of the most important
films I've seen this year!"
—ROGER EBERT, *Chicago Sun-Times*

AL FREEMAN, JR.   PHYLICIA RASHAD   LEON

BET PICTURES PRESENTS

ONCE UPON A TIME...
WHEN WE WERE COLORED

Butch Lewis

With the UIE production of *Once Upon a Time*, Reid made his feature-film directorial debut. The film was based on the book of the same title by Clifton Taulbert. Set in Mississippi in 1946, *Once Upon a Time* chronicles the author's coming-of-age in the segregated South when the Ku Klux Klan terrorized the streets and "Whites Only" were among the first words that African-American children learned. Taulbert was encouraged by the love and kinship of his tightly knit community to overcome Southern bigotry and intolerance. "It is a timeless, bittersweet love story," Reid says. "It is a warm, family film."

"It is important that everyone realizes that in most cases in the African-American community, young Black men and women set their sights, hopes and dreams on becoming a success mainly through athletics or entertainment," Lewis says. "Twenty years ago, Johnson took his dream, borrowed $15,000 and now has a $2 billion company—overseeing numerous publications and combined efforts in filmmaking. He's also employing and setting a platform for young Black executives in a field that would not normally be open to them. That is very important—and I always say to Johnson, that the harder he's worked, the luckier he's gotten."

A BROADER FORAY INTO ENTERTAINMENT

For the 1990-1991 season, BET continued to expand its original programming with the premiere of five new shows: "Live From L.A.," the network's first Los Angeles-based show; "Sound & Style With Ramsey Lewis"; "Kimboo"; "Family Figures"; and "Screen Scene."

"Live From L.A." was BET's foray into the entertainment talk-show arena. It featured celebrity guests, live musical performances, comedy sketches—all before a studio audience.

In 1990, BET split into two operating groups: the Entertainment Group and the Publishing Group. The Publishing Group began that November. At a news conference, BET announced its plans to publish *YSB,* the country's first informative, general-interest magazine for African-American teenagers and young adults. The first issue was published in August 1991 and was promoted largely on the network. BET ceased publishing *YSB* in 1996.

"Even though *YSB* is not around, I thought it was one of the best teen magazines out," Sheila Johnson, BET executive vice president of corporate affairs, says. "I think there is room out there for a really wholesome, outstanding, African-American teen magazine. It should be there to reach our youth."

BET added a second magazine in 1991, when it acquired Time Warner's interest in *Emerge,* an issue-oriented publication that provided news, commentary and analysis. *Time* magazine reporter Wilmer C. Ames Jr. started the magazine and published its first issue in 1988. Envisioned as a newsmagazine for African-Americans, Ames took on two new partners, BET and Syndicated Communications Inc., which jointly held 28.5 percent interest in the magazine. *Emerge* officially launched in October 1989. Soon after BET gained control of *Emerge*—it now owns 100 percent of the magazine—George E. Curry was appointed editor-in-chief.

Before taking over *Emerge's* top position, Curry served as New York bureau chief and a Washington correspondent for *The Chicago Tribune.*

YSB Premiere Issue

WALL STREET BOUND

The significant milestone, signaling BET was shifting gears into hyper-drive, came on September 18, 1991, with the formation of BET Holdings as the parent company. In November, Johnson

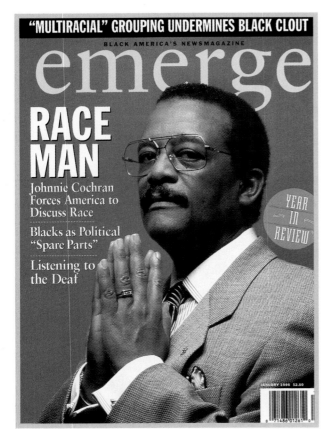

announced BET would go public, becoming the nation's first Black-owned company to offer stock on the New York Stock Exchange.

"When we went public, Bob and all our executive vice presidents entered the floor of the Exchange," Debra L. Lee, president and chief operating officer says, of the historic day. "All of the Black runners left whatever they were doing and came running to give us high fives. We were the first Blacks in that position. It was wonderful, and we were all very proud." BET's shares rose 39 percent on the first trading day, valuing the company at $475 million. "We got the funding we needed to start magazines, other cable networks and much of what BET has evolved into," Lee says.

In the early 1990s, as BET continued building strategic alliances and starting new businesses, the cable network remained the centerpiece, while the news and public affairs programming started to attract serious attention. In April 1990, "Conversations With Ed Gordon" scored the first of several historic and exclusive interviews, including a talk with former Washington Mayor Marion Barry Jr. from the federal prison in Loreto, Pennsylvania. It was the first interview Barry had granted since being incarcerated for illegal drug use. Other coups were interviews with Minister Louis Farrakhan of

New York Stock Exchange

the Nation of Islam and O.J. Simpson after his acquittal in his infamous "trial of the century."

"BET News" drew accolades from "The Verdict and the Violence," an acclaimed special examining the 1992 Los Angeles riots that erupted following the controversial acquittal of four L.A. police officers for viciously beating Rodney King. The four White officers were caught on video. And in May, BET aired another exclusive interview, this one with President George Bush, as part of its "Conversations With Ed Gordon" series. It was Bush's first television interview following his return from surveying the Los Angeles rebellion.

That fall, BET premiered several new shows, including "ComicView," which showcases up-and-coming comedians. Other new programs were "Love Between the Sexes," a match-making game featuring African-American singles, and "For Black Men Only," a discussion program for African-American men. Sports and children's programming continued to expand with the addition of "Sports Overtime," a live show featuring Black college sporting events, and "StoryPorch," a children's program designed to foster a love for books. In addition, "Triple Threat," a fast-paced, 30-minute game show, tested contestants' musical knowledge.

President George Bush

BET on Wheels

On BET's 13th anniversary in 1993, the network registered a 0.7 prime-time rating for the fourth quarter of 1992. This was the network's highest ever quarterly, prime-time rating.

Capitalizing on the nation's fascination with professional basketball, BET and NBA Entertainment, a division of the National Basketball Association, announced the premiere of "Converse/NBA Off the Court." The six-week series focused on the lives of past and present basketball superstars off the playing court.

CONSOLIDATION IS KEY

In May 1993, BET broke ground for its new corporate headquarters in northeast Washington. At this time, BET's offices were scattered throughout Washington and Northern Virginia.

Concerned about conditions of disharmony in Black communities throughout the nation, BET unveiled "Unity in the Community," a community-service campaign, on June 7, 1993, at the National Cable Television Association convention in San Francisco. The national promotion was anchored by BET on Wheels, a truck that converted into an 896-square-foot performance stage. BET kicked off this tour with its first "Unity Day" celebration in Oakland, California. BET on Wheels traveled to many locations that summer, with free concerts by such artists as Colin England, Nikita Germaine and Biz Markie. Speakers discussed health issues affecting the community, economic development and literacy.

Ossie Davis

Also at the NCTA Convention, BET said it would purchase 80 percent of Action Pay-Per-View from Avalon Communications Inc. The two-year-old, satellite-delivered movie channel was available all day to five million homes. Renamed BET Action Pay-Per-View, the acquisition allowed BET to increase distribution in urban locations, to enhance its advertising sales through cross-channel promotions and to create the first vehicle to distribute films for Black audiences.

By BET's 14th anniversary, the company reached 39.1 million homes, according to Nielsen Media Research. "Teen Summit," a one-hour teen talk show focusing on issues that affect young people, received an NAACP Image Award for its show on "Teens and AIDS." ""Teen Summit" is the brightest star of which I'm most proud," says Sheila Johnson, executive vice president of corporate affairs. "It has been able to send a positive message to the youth in America."

President Bill Clinton

BET was also recognized in 1994 as one of the "101 Corporate Heroes" by Childhelp USA and members of the United States Senate for its commitment to offering programming that positively impacts children and their families. The award specifically cited "Teen Summit," as well as "StoryPorch," which had captured the imagination of young children through captivating folk tales narrated by Bill Cosby, Maya Angelou, Ruby Dee, Ossie Davis, Edward James Olmos and other guests.

Another highlight came on November 2, 1994, with the presentation of "President Clinton and Black Americans: Face-to-Face." This special addressed concerns of importance to the Black community with a panel of African-American citizens.

The themes of freedom and the Black struggle were brought into the contemporary world when BET held a Nelson Mandela Freedom Fund Telethon to support South Africa's change to a democratic form of government. "Everyone from Danny Glover to Denzel Washington to Sidney Poitier appeared," says Cindy Mahmoud, former vice president of programming and specials. "It was an incredible experience."

Nelson Mandela

FACES OF BET

Current Hosts of BET's Popular Programs

CITA, Jam Zone

BOBBY JONES, Bobby Jones Gospel

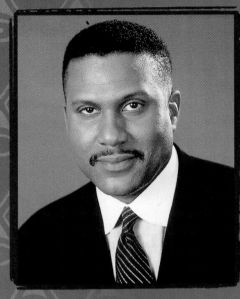

TAVIS SMILEY,
BET Tonight With Tavis Smiley

CHERYL MARTIN, BET News

GEORGE CURRY, Lead Story

BIG TIGGER, Rap City

LIZA MICHELLE, All   **ED GORDON, BET** News

MICHAEL COLYAR,
BET Live From L.A.

RACHEL,
BET Live From L.A.

SABRINA DAMES, BET News

HITS, Hits From The Street

ADIMU, Teen Summit

FRAN TOLLIVER,
Teen Summit

DR. RO, Heart & Soul

MOCHA LEE, Heart & Soul

LESTER BARRIE, ComicView

ANGELA STRIBLING, SHERRY CARTER, HERBIE HANCOCK, RAMSEY LEWIS and LOU RAWLS, BET on Jazz

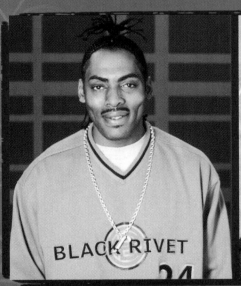

COOLIO, Madd Sports

LEM BARNEY,
Black College Football

CHARLIE NEAL, BET Sports

MALONDA, Out the Box

GERARD HENRY, Lift Every Voice

FUTURE BRIGHT

Since its creation just 20 years ago, BET has become the premier provider of African-American entertainment content. Bob Johnson has successfully expanded the BET brand to include not only television programming, but also film, restaurants, publishing and the Internet. As a result, BET has become a driving force in bringing African-American culture and programming to a large and ever-growing audience.

—Kenneth I. Chenault, President and COO,
American Express Company

celebrating twenty years

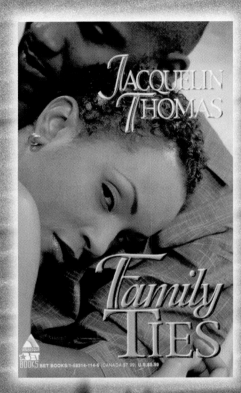

JACQUELIN
THOMAS

Family
Ties

BET
BOOKS SET BOOKS 1-58314-114-8 (CANADA $7.99) U.S. $5.99

95·00

1995

March

BET opens its six-story corporate headquarters in northeast Washington.

"BET News" broadcasts from the site of the 30th anniversary of the Civil Rights March from Selma to Montgomery.

April

BET opens Studio 2, a 58,000-square-foot film and video production facility, which can be leased for major motion picture and television production ventures.

June

BET Film Productions and United Image Entertainment premiere their first film, *Out of Sync*.

August

BET's "A Tribute to Black Music Legends" is nominated for an Emmy Award.

September

"BET News," *Emerge* and the AT&T Corporation present "Prescription for Change: the Health of Black America."

The Congressional Black Caucus Foundation and BET present "A National Town Hall Meeting: A Matter of Race."

BET inaugurates the BET Walk of Fame by honoring Michael Jackson.

November

BET Holdings Inc. announces an agreement to buy 3,036,600 common shares from Time Warner Inc., at an aggregate cost of $58 million.

BET Holdings Inc. makes *Forbes* magazine's listing of 200 Best Small Companies in America.

1995—Historic Highlights

"The Trial of the Century" ends as O.J. Simpson is acquitted of double-murder charges in Los Angeles.

The Million Man March is held on The Mall in Washington.

1996

January

BET on Jazz: The Cable Jazz Channel™ launches with a six-hour simulcast on BET network.

BET airs the first interview with O.J. Simpson after his acquittal.

February

BET launches *BET Weekend* magazine.

BET Holdings enters a venture with the Microsoft Corporation to develop MSBET.

March

Debra L. Lee is appointed President and Chief Operating Officer.

September

Whitney Houston becomes the second artist to be inducted into the BET Walk of Fame.

BET Movies/STARZ!3, a venture with the Encore Media Corporation, announces the nation's first 24-hour Black movie channel.

23 million subscribers

17.4 million subscribers

1989

3.8 million subscribers

1984

1986

8 million subscribers

ON AIR

ROBERT JOHNSON

January **1980**

1996—Historic Highlights

U.S. Secretary of Commerce Ronald H. Brown, 54, and members of his delegation are killed in an airplane crash in Croatia.

Willie Brown, 62, is sworn in as the first African-American mayor of San Francisco.

U.S. Representative Kweisi Mfume, 48, a Maryland Democrat, leaves Congress to head the NAACP.

January

BET SoundStage opens in Largo, Maryland.

October

Kenneth "Babyface" Edmonds, 38, is inducted into the BET Walk of Fame.

1997—Historic Highlights

Venus Williams, 17, plays in the finals of the U.S. Open Tennis Tournament.

Coleman A. Young, 79, former mayor of Detroit, dies.

May

BET acquires *Heart & Soul*, a health, fitness and beauty magazine.

60+ million subscribers

39.1 million subscribers

1994

2000

John H. Johnson, founder of the Johnson Publishing Company in Chicago, and Civil Rights pioneer Rosa Parks receive the presidential Medal of Freedom.

Kofi Annan, 58, a Ghanian diplomat, becomes the first Black African to serve as Secretary-General of the United Nations.

Ella Fitzgerald, "The First Lady of Song," dies at 78.

Rapper and actor Tupac Shakur, 25, is gunned down in Las Vegas.

Rapper Notorious B.I.G., 24, is murdered.

Betty Shabazz, 61, dies.

Alexis M. Herman, 50, is appointed U.S. Secretary of Labor. Rodney E. Slater, 41, is named U.S. Secretary of Transportation. Eric H. Holder Jr., 46, is confirmed as U.S. Deputy Attorney General.

William E. Kennard, 40, is appointed chairman of the Federal Communications Commission.

Tiger Woods, 21, wins the Masters golf tournament.

Kenneth I. Chenault, 46, is appointed President and Chief Executive Officer of the American Express Company.

June

BET Holdings acquires Arabesque Books from Kensington Publishing Inc.

BET on Jazz Restaurant opens in downtown Washington.

July

BET SoundStage Club opens at Downtown Disney Pleasure Island at Walt Disney World in Orlando, Florida.

BET shareholders approve the buyout of BET Holdings by Robert L. Johnson and the Liberty Media Group, taking the company private.

October

BET honors Boyz II Men on the BET Walk of Fame.

"Teen Summit" holds the first of three town hall meetings with the Kaiser Foundation.

The Artist Formerly Known as Prince breaks his legendary silence on "BET Tonight With Tavis Smiley."

Prince

1998—Historic Highlights

Julian Bond, 58, is appointed Chairman of NAACP's Board of Directors.

Michael Jordan leads the Chicago Bulls to their sixth NBA title.

1999

January

Tavis Smiley, host of "BET Tonight With Tavis Smiley," interviews Cuba's President Fidel Castro.

March

Robert L. Johnson receives the President's Award from the International Association of Jazz Educators.

June

Trés Jazz restaurant opens at the Paris Las Vegas Casino Resort.

August

BET and partners Microsoft Corporation, Liberty Digital LLC, News Corporation Inc. and USA Networks Inc. create BET.com, a new Internet portal.

October

Diana Ross is inducted into the BET Walk of Fame.

November

BET joins the Rock and Roll Hall of Fame and Museum in Cleveland to kick off the first hip-hop exhibit.

December

Vice President Al Gore appears on BET's "Lead Story."

Donnie Simpson returns to participate in a countdown of BET's "Top 100 Videos of the Century."

Serena and Venus Williams

1999—Historic Highlights

Lauryn Hill, 23, sweeps the Grammy Awards with her solo debut, *The Miseducation of Lauryn Hill*.

Serena Williams, 18, wins the U.S. Open Tennis Tournament.

FUTURE BRIGHT

I n 1995, BET celebrated 15 years with "The Big 15 Kickoff Jam" featuring CeCe Penniston and Lords of the Underground in a combination studio party and concert. During Black History Month, Rhino Records released *Black Entertainment Television's 15th Anniversary Music Celebration*, a two-volume collection commemorating the network's pioneering role in the record industry.

In March of that year, BET consolidated its vast operations under one roof in a six-story corporate headquarters building adjacent to BET's Network Operations facility. The following month, BET opened Studio 2, a state-of-the-art film and video production center. Clients that have used the center include Hollywood Pictures, which distributed the Demi Moore film *G.I. Jane*; Consumer News and Business Channel (CNBC); Mercury Records and Warner Brothers Records. In partnership with AT&T Corporation, BET also used the center to kick off a quarterly series of live town hall meetings, beginning in April 1995 with a 90-minute forum, "Silence Equals Death: AIDS in the Black Community."

Debra L. Lee

BET HONORS THE MUSIC

The town hall meetings were not the only memorable events of 1995. Other programs that year included two original episodes of "Lyrically Speaking," highlighting the music of Stevie Wonder and Patti LaBelle. "Music Inside Out" focused on the power brokers of Black music, along with Atlantic Records recording artist Brandy, singer Christopher Williams and Grammy-winning composer Gordon Chambers. Such music legends as Curtis Mayfield, Barry White and Aretha Franklin appeared on "Video Soul,"

BET Corporate Headquarters

while Berry Gordy and Bob Jones, the "Godfather of Black Hollywood," were featured on "Conversations With Ed Gordon."

"A Tribute to Black Legends" honored the lasting contributions of Louis Armstrong, Josephine Baker, Marvin Gaye and Billie Holiday. Produced by Baruch Entertainment, and hosted by Phylicia Rashad and Robert Townsend, this one-hour special was nominated for an Emmy Award.

BET's star shined even brighter that year, as BET Holdings made *Forbes* magazine's annual list of the "200 Best Small Companies in America" on November 15, 1995.

More accolades came in 1996 when O.J. Simpson granted "Conversations With Ed Gordon" his first full interview after his acquittal on murder charges. Simpson told Gordon that he was "as innocent as anyone else out there." He further stated that the media played a huge part in tainting America's perception of him. "The media is the main reason why America is feeling the way they're feeling," Simpson said. "They were lied to."

The Simpson interview delivered BET its highest Nielsen rating ever—6.9. It was nominated for an Emmy in 1997. "Getting Simpson to agree to an interview was tough," says Deborah Tang. "We, like a lot of people, were sending him letters and notes and cards and trying very hard to get the interview. What ultimately got BET the interview was that when O.J. Simpson came out, people saw—and he saw—that he was not going to get a 'warm fuzzy' from anybody—anybody. I think he just felt that the best shake he could get could come from us."

The Simpson interview was just one of many highlights of 1996—an extremely busy year for BET. The company made significant inroads in jazz, publishing and cyber-space through new cable channels, acquisitions and partnerships. BET on Jazz: The Cable Jazz Channel hit high notes with its six-hour debut simulcast on January 15, 1996. The programming included performances by saxophonist Joshua Redman, pianist

Ed Gordon

Elaine Elias and blues greats Muddy Waters and John Lee Hooker. BET on Jazz International was launched on June 1, 1996.

"Our vision is for BET on Jazz: The Jazz Channel to be a one-stop destination for anything jazz-related," says senior vice president Paxton Baker.

As the first television-programming service dedicated exclusively to jazz, BET on Jazz has been credited with re-igniting interest in the music, along with the tireless advocacy of trumpeter Wynton Marsalis and jazz radio stations around the country. And this interest has been fueled around the world with the launch of BET on Jazz International. Over the years, jazz lovers

BET on Jazz Performances

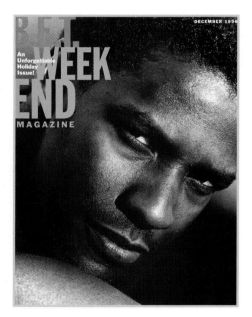

have seen such programs as "Jazz Central," the only daily, nationally televised program devoted exclusively to jazz. Hourlong concerts feature the music of Dr. Billy Taylor, Dave Brubeck, Roy Hargrove and Charlie Byrd, while Herbie Hancock offers inside information on concert tours, CD reviews, artist interviews and studio performances on "Jazz Scene."

Just weeks after BET unveiled its jazz programming, it took a major step into the world of publishing with the launch of *BET Weekend* at a star-studded gala that featured Academy Award-winning actor Denzel Washington, Leon, Mary Wilson of the Supremes and many others. *BET Weekend*, initially a joint venture with the *New York Daily News*, had the largest launch of any Black publication as a quarterly with a distribution of 800,000 in daily newspapers and Black-owned weeklies. "We tried to make sure it wasn't an ordinary supplement," explains Yanick Rice Lamb, editorial director of *BET Weekend* and *Heart & Soul*. "We wanted something that would rise out of the clutter of some of the newspapers on Sunday and give African-Americans what they deserved: a well-designed magazine that used the top writers, the top photographers and the top illustrators." The lifestyles, arts and entertainment magazine has been so well received that it's now the second-largest publication targeted to African-Americans, with a circulation of 1.3 million.

BET'S NEW WAVE

The dramatic evolution of BET continued when its board of directors appointed Debra L. Lee president and chief operating officer on March 19, 1996. Prior to her appointment, she held several posts, including general counsel and executive vice president of strategic business development. Lee holds a Harvard University law degree and master's degree from the John F. Kennedy School of Government. "I don't think there's a Black woman in the country who's higher ranking in authority than Debra Lee," Johnson says.

With Lee and Johnson at the helm, BET Holdings announced in 1996 that it would launch a new network with the Encore Media Corporation. In February 1997, BET Movies/ Starz![3] was the nation's first 24-hour movie channel devoted to showcasing Black film artists.

BET opened a new chapter in the book-publishing arena in 1998 with the purchase of Arabesque Books, the first line of original African-American romance novels, from Kensington

Arabesque Films' cast
and author of *Incognito*

Publishing Company. The property included an extensive list of 200 titles, the Arabesque Book Club and the dramatic rights to Arabesque book titles for television and film development.

BET kicked off the Arabesque film series on Friday, September 17, 1999, with the world premiere of the edgy romantic thriller *Incognito*, based on the book by best-selling author Francis Ray. Acclaimed filmmaker Julie Dash (*Daughters of the Dust*) was the director. Other films were *Intimate Betrayal*, *Rendezvous*, *After All*, *Rhapsody*, *Masquerade* and *Midnight Blue*. The films starred, among others, Holly Robinson Peete and Kim Fields.

Forming BET Arabesque Films is a significant milestone in BET's history. And in 1998, Johnson and Liberty Media Corporation, headed by his original partner, John Malone, brought the com-

pany full circle when they privatized BET Holdings for $63 a share. The final purchase price was estimated at $400 million. Although going public in 1991 was one of Johnson's most memorable experiences, "the day we went private was pretty exciting, too," he says.

A TALENTED TEAM

Even with all of his successes, Johnson counts himself most fortunate in BET's ability to attract a corps of Black managerial talent. "I'm most proud of those who have been a part of BET, the people who have succeeded in life with BET," he says. "Not just

Songs popularized on
"Video Soul" and featured
on the Rhino Records box set
*Black Entertainment Television's
15th Anniversary Music Celebration.*

"Superwoman" by Karyn White

"Gangsta Lean" by K.R.S.-One

"I'm Ready" by Tevin Campbell

"Being With You"
     by Smokey Robinson

"Celebration" by Kool & The Gang

"Freeway of Love"
     by Aretha Franklin

"Looking For A New Love"
     by Jody Watley

"Give It To Me Baby" by Rick James

"Nite and Day" by Al. B. Sure

BET Music Family

the people who work at BET, but also the celebrities who have appeared on BET—the talent in the music videos and artists that started out as baby acts and are now superstars. I'm also proud of all of the other people who have been a part of BET and have gone on to new and successful careers."

BET has been a career springboard for a variety of employees, including Ed Gordon, who was lured away by MSNBC soon after the O.J. Simpson interview (Gordon will return to BET in Fall 2000); James Brown, the Fox-TV sportscaster and home-video show host; former "Teen Summit" host Ananda Lewis, now a popular MTV VJ; and D.L. Hughley, former "Comic-View" host and now star of his own sit-com.

Executives at BET are able to stretch in ways unmatched at other companies. "Bob has allowed me to build my own structure," says Executive Vice President of affiliate sales and marketing Curtis N. Symonds, who left ESPN in 1988 to join BET. Having started with five employees he now has 40. "I don't know if that opportunity would have existed anywhere else—to run your own shop."

Kelli Richardson, who joined BET in 1996 after leaving Procter & Gamble, has been senior vice president of corporate marketing and communications since 1999. "BET has created some wonderful original programming that we have been able to market to the consumer very differently than we have done in the past," she says. "What's been most exciting for me is being able to come in and develop a holistic plan that includes traditional and alternative vehicles to get our message across. Music programming will always be our core, but it's not everything BET has to offer."

Stephen Hill joined BET in June 1999 after working at MTV as director of music programming. As vice president of music programming, Hill oversees music shows such as "Rap City: Tha Bassment," "Hits From The Street," "Midnight Love" and "Jam Zone," which has a virtual-reality homegirl, Cita, as host. "The challenge for Cita is maintaining a three-dimensional personality," Hill says. "She's not all about the dis, and she's not all about the love. She has loves and hates. And the great thing is that people respond to her like she's a real person. She gets letters, she gets phone calls. It's great."

Another leader who has helped to define BET's culture is George E. Curry. As editor-in-chief of *Emerge*, he has won more than 15 national journalism awards. "Bob Johnson has never asked me to shy away from controversy or go easy on Black leaders—even if they were his friends," Curry wrote in the February 2000 issue of *Emerge*.

"In addition to respecting our professionalism at *Emerge*, Bob Johnson did something else that I'll always admire," Curry continued. "When organizers of the Million Man March were being attacked, and our leaders were being urged to distance themselves from Minister Louis Farrakhan, Bob Johnson did not buckle. In addition to providing free air time on BET for march supporters—and broadcasting portions of the Million Man March as well—the CEO closed down BET's corporate headquarters in support of the effort, took out a full-page ad in a national newspaper to declare his support for the event and was among the million who assembled at the foot of the Capitol. What other corporate executive, Black or White, did that?"

Russell Simmons also salutes Johnson for his support of the Million Man March. "BET has been the only voice, entertainment voice, that has had a constant and thorough impact on the community," Simmons says. "From a cultural standpoint, they have been able to help globalize the urban culture—and they have been the greatest tool for marketing all of the ideas out of the urban community. They have been influential and as much a part of developing culture in mainstream America as any other vehicle. And the biggest evidence is their support of the Million Man March and how successful that was."

Million Man March

"Taking BET back to the streets is the key to maintaining that connection," says Curtis Gadson, vice president of programming. "We want to be as close to our audience as possible. We want our talent and producers out there with the viewers, so we can find out what they want to see on the air and give it to them."

The mix for the 1999-2000 season includes: "All," "Morning Moves," "BET Videolink," "Hits From The Street," "Jam Zone," "Rap City: Tha Bassment," "Midnight Love," "Bobby Jones Gospel" and "Video Gospel." Other programs on this season's schedule are "Madd Sports" with Coolio, "Heart & Soul," "Black College Sports," "ComicView," hosted by Lester Barrie with Reynaldo Ray, and an updated "BET Live From L.A.," hosted by Michael Colyar and Rachel. The news and public affairs mainstays include "Teen Summit," "BET Tonight With Tavis Smiley" and "Lead Story."

Russell Simmons

A TASTE OF SOUL

BET took its first step into the restaurant industry with BET SoundStage Restaurant, the first of four such BET operations. Located in Largo, Maryland, near Mitchell-ville, one of the wealthiest Black communities in America, the restaurant opened officially in January 1997. Its opening night drew such celebrities as Aretha Franklin, Boyz II Men and Babyface.

BET SoundStage seats 360 and treats patrons to a multimedia experience. Behind a computerized hostess stand two tiers of video-and-sound control panels enclosed in a glass booth. Strategically situated throughout SoundStage are 42 television monitors, large and small. They showcase the hottest, as well as classic, music videos. Black stage lights and cameras hang from a metal ceiling grid, giving diners the feel of being in a stage production.

BET furthered its brand identity with the unveiling of remaining restaurants: BET SoundStage Club, at Walt Disney World Resort in Orlando, Florida, and BET on Jazz Restaurant in downtown Washington. Both opened in 1998.

The BET SoundStage Club opened in June 1998 as a unique dance club, providing state-of-the-art multimedia displays of music and video. This sensational waterfront club features the best of jazz, rhythm and blues, soul and hip-hop. The club, the first of its kind on Disney property, is seen as a cornerstone in Disney's attempt to court African-Americans. Its red-carpet gala on opening night attracted many corporate executives, along with a phalanx of entertainers, including Destiny's Child, Jagged Edge and Xscape, as well as actors Malik Yoba, Leon and Robert Townsend, and basketball player Anfernee "Penny" Hardaway. That summer also marked the opening of BET on Jazz Restaurant, where Johnson sought to combine two passions—his love for great food and great music. The restaurant features New World Caribbean cuisine amid elegant art-deco surroundings. The experience is enhanced by the diverse appeal of BET on Jazz programming and live entertainment on weekends.

Trés Jazz opened in 1999 in the Paris Las Vegas Resort Casino in Las Vegas as the only jazz-themed establishment on The Strip. Trés Jazz blends an enticing menu of New World Caribbean cuisine with distinctive continental fare. The menu was inspired by Miami chef and restauranteur Cindy Hutson, who also created the menu for BET on Jazz Restaurant in Washington. Patrons enjoy live jazz performances in a beautiful art-deco setting reminiscent of a Parisian supper club.

BET SoundStage Restaurant

BET on Jazz Restaurant

Trés Jazz Restaurant

BET MOVES FORWARD AND CONTENT RULES

"If there's one thing that you're going to see within the next five years it is a heavy emphasis on content, a heavy emphasis on brand marketing," Johnson predicts. "We think that will yield the greatest value. Clearly, we will go public again."

A significant portion of this content will come from the magazines—*BET Weekend, Emerge* and *Heart & Soul*, which was purchased from Rodale, a Pennsylvania-based publishing company, in May 1998. Johnson is poised to become the biggest publisher of African-American magazines as part of an investment and publishing deal with Keith Clinkscales, the former publisher of *Vibe*. Under the agreement, Clinkscales, who runs Vanguarde Media, assumed the day-to-day management of BET's magazines. BET and equity investment fund Provender Capital became significant shareholders in Clinkscales' closely held publishing enterprise, which includes *Honey*, a multicultural magazine targeted to young women, and *Impact*, an entertainment trade publication. The venture has a combined circulation of more than 2 million with the prospect for future growth through acquisitions and start-ups.

Another exciting venture is the recently launched BET.com, the ultimate Internet portal for African-Americans with broad, in-depth and timely content, as well as e-commerce. The venture was created with $35 million from BET and four of America's largest communications companies: Microsoft Corporation, Liberty Digital LLC, News Corporation Inc. and USA Networks Inc.

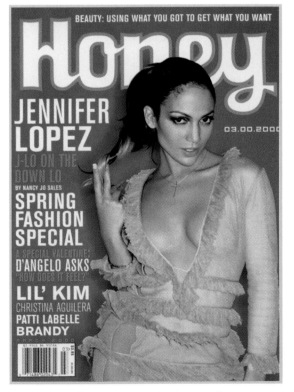

"Our primary mission to the consumer is to provide interactive media and services that educate, enrich, empower and entertain African-Americans," says Scott Mills, chief operating officer of BET.com. "Our corporate mission is to become the leading African-American Web site."

"Across the nine channels, we have Sports, which we categorize broadly as headlines, and then we have Money, Lifestyles, Music, Health, Food, Careers and BET corporate," Mills explains. "We also created zones, such as an urban zone, a professional zone, a women's zone and a family zone."

BET.com represents the largest investment yet to target the largely overlooked Black online market. The Web portal has been hailed by NAACP President Kweisi Mfume for attempting to bridge the "digital divide." According to a report by the United States Commerce Department, only 11.2 percent of African-American households have regular access to the Internet, compared to

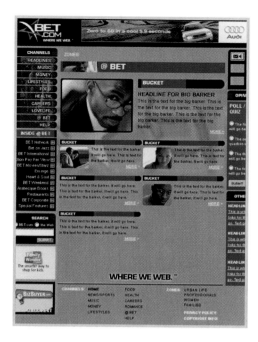

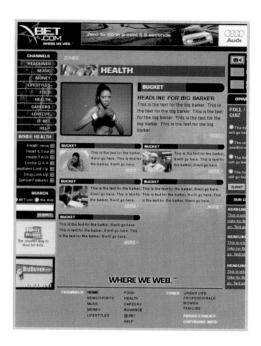

29.8 percent of White homes. "The hardware divide is solvable," Johnson says. "What I'm more concerned about is the attitudinal divide: Right now, African-Americans think, 'There's nothing on the Internet that's of value to me.'"

"The biggest thing we're looking at right now is BET.com," he adds. "That has the potential to be as big as BET. In the next five years it should just grow by leaps and bounds. The other big push right now is on the movie side, with BET Pictures II, not only the made-for-TV movies that we started, but also the theatrical releases. That's a wide-open area. We've also been getting good feedback on jazz and that's just going to grow. We've been looking at the other networks—the magazines and everything we do in terms of just pushing the content—the dot-com."

Looking back over the last 20 years, Sheila Johnson feels a mix of love, pride and astonishment. "I'm very proud of my husband for what he has created," she says. "He's done one hell of a job. I look at the network every day with pride and in some ways disbelief."

"BET is arguably the most successful Black business in the world," Bob Johnson adds. "It has created a brand that I think will last forever. It has impacted a lot of people's lives. The most exciting thing about it is that it ain't through yet. We've got a lot of stuff to do!"

Robert L. Johnson

BET has harnessed new technologies to entertain millions, but
also to enlighten, educate and eliminate bias and barriers in
the media, marketplace and in the mind of America. Certainly,
progress begins with knowledge. BET's effort to help families
understand how to achieve the American dream . . . is crucial
to advancing economic equality.

—**FRANKLIN D. RAINES,** Chairman and CEO,
Fannie Mae

HOT PROPERTIES

BET HOLDINGS INC.

is the center of a constellation of multiple businesses dedicated to utilizing, illuminating and continuing to build the BET brand name for the delivery of entertainment, information, merchandise and leisure-time activity to the growing Black consumer market.

BET INC.

owns and operates Black Entertainment Television, an advertiser-supported basic cable television network that is its core business. Launched in January 1980, the network serves as both a cultural center and information source for Black consumers. The BET network airs a variety of music, news, sports and public affairs shows, as well as originally produced and syndicated programming, 24 hours a day to more than 60 million cable households.

BET.COM

is an African-American Internet portal offering content for all ages including news, sports, entertainment, music, education, health, finance, careers and travel. The site also has e-commerce, e-mail and interactive chat communities. A joint venture between BET Holdings and Microsoft Corporation, Liberty Digital LLC, News Corporation Inc. and USA Networks Inc., BET.COM launched in February 2000. BET has majority ownership and control of the venture.

BET ARABESQUE FILMS

(BET Arabesque LLC) is a movie production entity created to produce films and made-for-TV movies about African-Americans. BET Arabesque Films has committed to the largest single production order of African-American feature-length films in Hollywood history. In March 1999, the company began production on 10 original made-for-TV movies based on Arabesque romance novels which began airing on BET in the fall of 1999.

BET PICTURES II

is one of the nation's first Black-owned movie studios created to produce African-American theatrical films. BET Pictures II was established in July of 1998.

TRÉS JAZZ RESTAURANT™

opened in September of 1999 within the new Paris Las Vegas Casino Resort. Patrons enjoy live jazz performances and a dining experience of New World Caribbean cuisine in a beautiful setting reminiscent of a Parisian supper club.

BET ON JAZZ RESTAURANT™

opened in June 1998, combines great food with great music. Located in downtown Washington, D.C., the restaurant features New World Caribbean cuisine in an elegant art-deco setting.

BET SOUNDSTAGE CLUB™

is a waterfront dance club that opened in June 1998, at Walt Disney World in Orlando, Florida. The club features the best of rhythm and blues and hip-hop performances, as well as programming from BET cable channels.

BET SOUNDSTAGE RESTAURANT™

is an entertainment-themed, high-tech restaurant that opened in January 1997 in Largo, Maryland, a suburb of Washington, D.C.

BET GOSPEL

is a new digital 24-hour inspirational network featuring the best in motivational speakers and gospel music.

HEART & SOUL

is a national health, fitness and beauty magazine that addresses the many issues facing African-American women today. The magazine was acquired in May 1998.

BET WEEKEND

is a Black-oriented entertainment and lifestyle magazine launched as a quarterly newspaper insert in February 1996. The publication became monthly in February 1997 and is the second largest Black publication with a circulation of 1.3 million.

EMERGE

is a hard news and public affairs magazine geared toward Black America. The magazine was launched in 1989.

ARABESQUE BOOKS

was purchased in June 1998. The African-American romance imprint includes an extensive list of 200 titles, the Arabesque Book Club and the dramatic rights to Arabesque books for television and film development.

BET ON JAZZ: THE JAZZ CHANNEL™

is the first 24-hour television programming service dedicated exclusively to jazz music. BET on Jazz features many of the finest jazz musicians through in-studio performances, festivals, concerts and celebrity interviews. Many programs feature original, as well as historic, footage unavailable on any other broadcast network.

BET ACTION PAY-PER-VIEW

is a 24-hour, satellite-delivered pay-per-view network owned and operated by BET Holdings Inc. The network showcases action, adventure, thriller movies, original programming and special events.

BET MOVIES/STARZ![3]

is a joint partnership with Encore Media Corporation that operates the nation's first 24-hour, urban-and Black-oriented movie channel devoted to showcasing Black actors. The channel was launched in February 1997.

BET INTERNATIONAL™

develops and coordinates the network's distribution of programming for BET and BET on Jazz: The Jazz Channel™ in 13 countries worldwide, including Africa, Europe, the Caribbean and Japan.

BOARD MEMBERS

Robert L. Johnson, Founder, Chairman & CEO

Debra L. Lee, President & COO

Sheila Johnson, EVP, Corporate Affairs

Robert Bennett, President & CEO, Liberty Media Corporation

John C. Malone, Ph.D., Chairman of the Board, Liberty Media Corporation

Denzel Washington, Actor

Herbert P. Wilkins Sr., President, Syncom Management

EXECUTIVE STAFF

Louis Carr - EVP, Media Sales

Byron Merchant - EVP, CAO & General Counsel

Scott Mills - EVP & COO, BET.com

Curtis Symonds - EVP, Affiliate Sales & Marketing

Paxton Baker - SVP & General Manager, BET on Jazz

Lee Chaffin - SVP, Affiliate Sales & Marketing

Curtis Gadson - SVP, Entertainment Programming

Raymond Goulbourne - SVP, Media Sales

Kelli Richardson - SVP, Corporate Marketing & Communications

PHOTO CREDITS

Photo credits are arranged by chapter.

Cover: 1. Robert L. Johnson by Kim Johnson, 2. Whitney Houston by Ruven Afanador/Outline, 3. Gladys Knight by Randy St. Nicholas/Outline, 4. Will Smith by Michael O'Neill/Outline, 5. Spike Lee by Anthony Barboza, 6. Issac Hayes by K. Alston/Outline, 7. Tina Turner by Herb Ritts/Virgin, 8. En Vogue by B. Malone/Retna, 9. Janet Jackson by A. Watson/Virgin, 10. Tim Reid & Daphne Maxwell Reid by BET, 11. George Curry by BET, 12. Nelson Mandela by A. Renault/Globe, 13. Snoop Doggy Dog by D. Ridgers/London Features, 14. Michael Jordan by L. Marano/London Features, 15. Denzel Washington by Pacha/Corbis, 16. Lauryn Hill by The Everett Collection, 17. Jazz musicians by BET, 18. Bob Marley by Art Slane/Sipa Press, 19. Herbie Hancock photo by Gouert De Roos/London Features, 20. Prince by Ron Wolfson/London Features, 21. Tupac Shakur by The Everett Collection, 22. Missy Elliott by Musto/London Features, 23. Mary J. Blige with Rachel by Andre Richardson, 24. Tavis Smiley by BET, 25. Queen Latifah by George Holtz/Corbis Outline, 26. Erykah Badu by J. Hicks/London Features, 27. Michael Jackson by Eugene Adebari/London Features, 28. Eve by Anthony Cutajar/London Features, 29. D'Angelo by Thierry Legoues/Virgin, 30. Kenneth "Babyface" Edmonds by Randee St. Nicholas/Outline.

Chapter 1: 1.Underworld by The Everett Collection, 2. College Football by BET, 3. Gospel Singer Bobby Jones by BET, 4. Bob Marley by Art Slane/Sipa Press, 5. Muhammad Ali by Stephen Harvey/Outline, 6. Michael Jackson Thriller by The Everett Collection, 7. Robert L. Johnson by Kim Johnson, 8. Bob Marley by Art Slane/Sipa Press, 9. Bobby Jones by BET, 10. Toni Morrison by BET, 11. Michael Jackson by David Fisher/London Features, 12. Carl Lewis by Chuck Muhlstock/Globe Photos, 13. Michael Jordan by Globe Photos, 14. Arthur Ashe by Soire En L'Honneur/Sipa Press, 15. Harry Belafonte by BET, 16. Oprah Winfrey by Anthony Dixon/London Features, 17. Wynton Marsalis by Carol Friedman/Outline, 18. Robert L. Johnson by BET, 19. John C. Malone by Chick Harrity/Corbis, 20. College Football by BET, 21. Underworld by The Everett Collection, 22. God's Stepchildren by Kisch/Photofest, 23. Emperor Jones by The Everett Collection, 24. Stormy Weather by The Everett Collection, 25. Bobby Jones by BET, 26. Bobby Jones/Choir by BET, 27. Shalamar by Ron Wolfson/London Features, 28. Midnight Starr by Ron Wolfson/London Features, 29. Earth, Wind & Fire by Globe Photos, 30. Run-DMC by John Barrett/Globe.

Special Section: BET's Top 100 Videos of the 20th Century: 1. Dr. Martin Luther King Jr. by Globe Photos, 2. Michael Jackson by Rex, 3. Busta Rhymes by K. Mazur/ London Features, 4. Marvin Gaye by Star File Photo, 5. Dr. Dre by Roger Erickson/Corbis Outline, 6. Run-DMC with Aerosmith by Chuck Pulin/Star File Photo, 7. TLC by J. Silverstein/Rex, 8. Janet Jackson by Rex, 9. M.C. Hammer by K. Mazur/London Features, 10. Herbie Hancock by Gouert De Roos/London Features, 11. Tupac Shakur by The Everett Collection, 12. D.J. Jazzy Jeff and Will Smith by Chris Booren Sunshine/Retna, 13. Notorious B.I.G. and Puffy Combs by Dennis Van Tine/London Features, Bone Thugs-n-Harmony by The Everett Collection, 15. The Artist Formerly Known As Prince by The Everett Collection, 16. Naughty by Nature by Steve Rapport/London Features, 17. N.W.A. by Derek Ridgers/London Features, 18. Earth, Wind & Fire by The Everett Collection, 19. LL Cool J by London Features, 20. Brandy and Monica by The Everett Collection, 21. Coolio by Bernhard Kuhmstedt/Retna, 22. George Clinton by Antoine LeGrand/Corbis Outline, 23. Grandmaster Flash by Janette Beckman/Retna, 24. Lionel Richie by P. Musto/London Features, 25. The Fugees by The Everett Collection, 26. New Edition by The Everett Collection, 27. Wreckx-N-Effect by The Everett Collection, 28. Boyz II Men by George Holz/Outline, 29. En Vogue by Brian Rasic/Rex, 30. R. Kelly by The Everett Collection, 31. Whitney Houston by Ruven Afanador/Outline, 32. DeBarge by The Everett Collection, 33. Will Smith by The Everett Collection, 34. Snoop Doggy Dogg by Tom Sheehan/London Features, 35. Missy Elliott by Musto/London Features, 36. Public Enemy by Edie Baskin/Outline, 37. D'Angelo by Thierry Legoues/Virgin, 38. Erykah Badu by J. Hicks/London Features, 39. Tina Turner by Herb Ritts/Virgin.

Chapter 2: 1. Teen Summit Group photo by BET, 2. Sherry Carter and Donnie Simpson by BET, 3. Spike Lee by Anthony Barboza, 4. Jesse Jackson by Kimberly Butler/London Features, 5. Whoopi Goldberg and Tavis Smiley by Ron Ceasar/BET, 6. Sherry Carter by BET, 7. Cheryl Martin by BET, 8. Florence Griffith-Joyner by Ron Wolfson/London Features, 9. Ron Brown by BET, 10. L. Douglas Wilder by John Barrett/Globe Photos, 11. Colin Powell by Lisa Quinones/Black Star, 12. Ed Gordon by BET, 13. Cheryl Martin by BET, 14. Ed Gordon with Ron Brown by BET, 15. Tavis Smiley with Vice President Al Gore by Ron Ceasar/BET, 16. Tavis Smiley by BET, 17. Bev Smith by BET, 18. Butch Lewis by Butch Lewis Productions, 19. Jesse Jackson by Paul Elledge/Outline.

Special Section: BET Walk of Fame: 1. Walk of Fame by Ron Ceasar/BET, 2. William Gray photo by UNCF/The Fund, 3. Michael Jackson photos by Outline Press, Musto/London Features, Streater/London Features and David Fisher/London Features, 4. Whitney Houston by Griffin/London Features,G. De Sota/London Features, Ruven Afanador/Outline, 5. Kenneth "Babyface" Edmonds by Randee St. Nicholas/Outline, Nick Elgar/London Features and Ron Wolfson/London Features, 6. Boyz II Men by George Holz/Outline, Frank Forcino/London Features and Dennis Van Tine/London Features, 7. Diana Ross by G. De Sota/London Features, Peter Freed/Corbis Outline, Frank Griffin/London Features, Ron Wolfson/London Features, 8. Sheila Johnson by BET.

Chapter 3: 1. D.L. Hughley by BET, 2. Bill Cosby by BET, 3. Man Laughing by BET, 4. Nelson Mandela by Mark Peters/Sipa Press, 5. *Emerge* cover by BET, 6. Once Upon A Time Poster courtesy of Butch Lewis Productions, 7. Quincy Jones by Larry Eusacca/Retna, 8. Denzel Washington by Armando Gallo/Retna, 9. Thurgood Marshall by Globe Photos, 10. Clarence Thomas by Dennis Brack/Black Star, 11. Terry McMillan by Ken Porbst/Outline, 12. Dr. Mae Jemison by Black Star, 13. Minister Louis Farrakhan by Alan Reingold, 14. Tim and Daphne Maxwell Reid by Joe Marzollo/Retna, 15. Butch Lewis by Butch Lewis Productions, 16. *Once Upon A Time* . . . poster courtesy of Butch Lewis Productions, 17. YSB cover by BET, 18. *Emerge* cover of Johnnie Cochran by BET, 19. *Emerge* layout by BET, 20. New York Stock Exchange by Andrea Renault/Globe Photos, 21. George Bush by Monwest/Globe Photos, 22. BET on Wheels by BET, 23. Ossie Davis by BET, 24. Nelson Mandela by Mark Peters/Sipa Press, 25. President Bill Clinton by Ron Ceasar.

Special Section: Faces of BET: All photos in this section are courtesy of BET, unless otherwise indicated. 1. Cita, 2. Bobby Jones by Bobby Jones, 3. Tavis Smiley, 4. Cheryl Martin, 5. George Curry, 6. Big Tigger, 7. Liza Michelle, 9. Michael Colyar by BET, 10. Rachel by Mike Ruiz/Visages, 11. Hits, 12. Adimu, 13. Dr. Ro, 14. Mocha Lee, 15. Coolio, 16. Lem Barney, 17. Charlie Neal by Welton B. Doby, 18. Malonda, 19. Gerard Henry, 20. Fran Tolliver by James Hicks, 21. Angela Stribling by Solid Image Photography, 22. Sherry Carter, 23. Ramsey Lewis, 24. Herbie Hancock by Jeffrey Newbury/Corbis Outline, 25. Lou Rawls by Jeff Slocumb/Corbis Outline, 26. Lester Barrie, 27. Sabrina Dames by Welton B. Doby.

Chapter 4: 1. Stevie Wonder by Star File, 2. A Tribute to Black Legends/Dancers by BET, 3. Family Ties - Arabesque Romance Cover by BET, 3. BET.com Homepage by BET, 4. *BET Weekend* cover - Angela Bassett by BET, 5. D'Angelo by Colin Streater/London Features, 6. Tina Turner and David Bowie by BET, 7. The Artist Formerly Known as Prince by Ron Wolfson/London Feature, 8. Debra Lee by BET, 9. BET Corporate Headquarters by BET, 10. Ed Gordon by BET, 11. BET on Jazz artists by BET, 12. Million Man March by Trippett/Sipa Press, 13. Russell Simmons by Barboza, 14. BET Music Family by BET, 15. Shrimp on plate by BET, 16. SoundStage by BET, 17. BET on Jazz restaurant by BET, 18. Trés Jazz by Jeffrey Green, 19. BET.com homepages by BET, 20. Serena and Venus Williams by Andrea Renault/Globe Photos, 21. Incognito courtesy The PR Squad, 22. Robert L. Johnson by Kim Johnson.

Every effort has been made by the Publisher to acknowledge all sources and copyrightholders. In the event of any copyrightholder being inadvertently omitted, please contact the Publisher directly.

ACKNOWLEDGEMENTS

BET BOOKS

wishes to acknowledge the following in development
and production of this book:

Kensington Publishing: Walter Zacharius, Steve Zacharius, Laurie Parkin, Paul Dinas and Karen Thomas. BET Holdings Inc.: Todd Beamon, Jacqueline Brooks, Wayne Burris, Michelle Curtis, Michael Freeman, Bobette Gillette, Margaret Johnson-Greene, Dandrea James Harris, Tracy Mackel, Tasha Price and Tiffani N. Taylor. Others who made this work possible: Augustus Jones, Cheryl Thompson, Constance M. Green, Dr. Joseph Cater and Julia Shaw.

COLOPHON

The headlines for *Black Star Power: BET Celebrating 20 Years*
are set in **CHIMES**, a contemporary display font that
celebrates this digital age of global communication.
The text is set in **Memphis**, an Egyptian revival
typeface designed in 1929 by
Dr. Rudolf Wolf. Egyptian revival faces
became popular in the United States in the 1880s. The
captions are set in **Gill Sans**, designed by British sculptor
Eric Gill between 1928 and 1930. Gill based his design on the
typeface created by Edward Johnson for the signage
in London's underground railway, the Tube.

celebrating twenty years

celebrating twenty years